We Celebrate
Family Days

Bobbie Kalman

Susan Hughes   Karen Harrison

The Holidays & Festivals Series

 Crabtree Publishing Company

The Holidays and Festivals Series
Created by Bobbie Kalman

Writing team:
Bobbie Kalman
Susan Hughes
Lise Gunby

Illustrations:
Pages 4-7, 10-11, 17, 22-23, 30-41, 46-55 by Karen Harrison
Pages 14-15, 18-21, 43, by Bernadette Lau
Pages 8, 12-13, 24-25, 28-29, 44-45 by Magda Markowski
© Crabtree Publishing Company

Editor-in-Chief:
Bobbie Kalman

Editors:
Susan Hughes
Lise Gunby
Dan Liebman
Catherine Johnston

Art direction:
Jane Hamilton
Susan Hughes
Catherine Johnston

Design and mechanicals:
Elaine Macpherson Enterprises Limited

For my mother

Cataloguing in Publication Data
Kalman, Bobbie, 1947-
    We celebrate family days

(The Holidays and festivals series)
Includes index.
ISBN 0-86505-048-1 (bound)
ISBN 0-86505-058-9 (pbk.)

1. Family festivals - Juvenile literature.
I. Hughes, Susan, 1960- . II. Harrison, Karen.
III. Title. IV. Series.

GT2420.K34 1986   j392   LC93-6181

350 Fifth Ave., Suite 3308
New York, N.Y. 10118

360 York Road, R.R.4
Niagara-on-the-Lake, Ontario L0S 1J0

73 Lime Walk
Headington, Oxford OX3 7AD

Contents

Our family gets together

Hurray! Today's the special day
That we have once a year.
It's our annual reunion
For family far and near.
Moms and dads, uncles and aunts,
Brothers and sisters, too,
Grandparents, in-laws, and cousins;
We all love our family "do!"

We eat and play and talk about
Those special family things,
Like Old Uncle Harold's missing teeth,
And the joy Baby Quentin brings,

4

And Granny's entry in the two-mile race,
And Sarah's graduation day,
And Great-Aunt Bessie's death last month,
And Robert's lead in the play.
We kid Michelle about her marriage plans
(It's her second wedding, you see),
And we help little Paul when his brand-new kitten
Gets stuck in the apple tree.

I love this annual tradition we have
Of sharing news and fun.
We're lucky to have one another to love.
It makes our family a happy one!

5

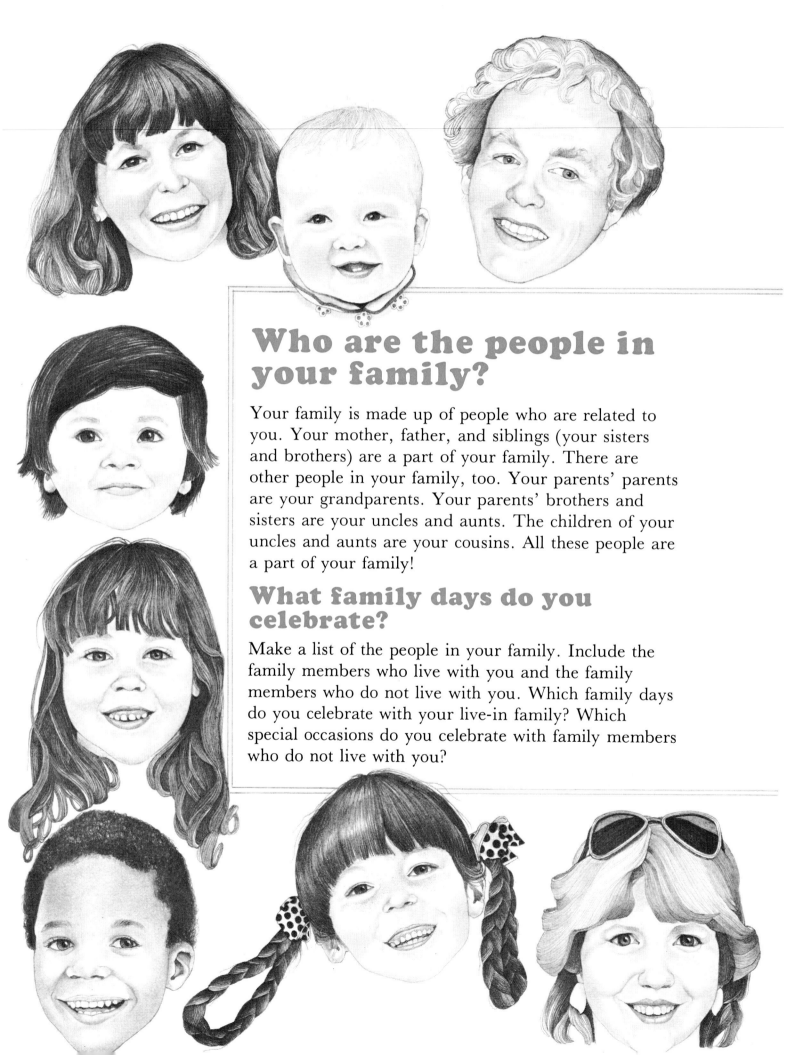

Who are the people in your family?

Your family is made up of people who are related to you. Your mother, father, and siblings (your sisters and brothers) are a part of your family. There are other people in your family, too. Your parents' parents are your grandparents. Your parents' brothers and sisters are your uncles and aunts. The children of your uncles and aunts are your cousins. All these people are a part of your family!

What family days do you celebrate?

Make a list of the people in your family. Include the family members who live with you and the family members who do not live with you. Which family days do you celebrate with your live-in family? Which special occasions do you celebrate with family members who do not live with you?

Changing families

In many countries around the world, the make-up of families today is different from that of fifty years ago. Many parents divorce. Children of divorced parents often live with just one of their parents. Sometimes siblings may live with different parents. Many parents remarry and form a new family with the children from their first marriage. Children who were not related before are now brothers and sisters! Although there are many combinations, any family can be a happy one as long as the family members care for one another.

Special thanks

Sometimes we forget that our family members are our friends. Sometimes we forget that it's fun to do something special for them. There are many days in the year when we can celebrate our family. We can say, "Thanks for everything you do for me. Thanks for being you!"

People around the world celebrate special days for their grandparents, parents, brothers, sisters, and children. These days help us to remember the people in our family. One of these days is Mother's Day.

Mother's Day

Mother's Day is an important day around the world. It is celebrated on different days in different countries. In France, Mother's Day is the last Sunday in May. In Spain, it is celebrated on December 8. In the United States, Canada, and several European countries, Mother's Day is the second Sunday in May.

Going a-mothering

The first Mother's Day was celebrated thousands of years ago. People who lived in a country called Phrygia believed in a goddess called Cybele. Cybele was the mother of all the gods and goddesses. Once a year, the Phrygians had a lively festival to honor Cybele.

In later days, Mothering Sunday was celebrated in Europe. Many children had to work in towns and villages far from their families. They had only one holiday each year. It was on a Sunday. On that Sunday, they walked home to see their mothers. Some of the children had to walk a very long way, but they did not mind. They were going "a-mothering."

A day of rest?

"It's Mother's Day! It's Mother's Day!" Petra and Sissy raced their brother Marek downstairs. "I'll get the card," said Petra. Sissy volunteered to bring the flowers. Meanwhile, Marek made the scrambled eggs, toast, and coffee. Laddy, the chocolate-brown mutt, knew something special was happening. He was so excited that he ran around everyone's legs.

Petra had everyone sign the card. Sissy put the flowers into a vase, and Marek placed the scrambled eggs, toast, and coffee on a silver tray.

The children called to their mother to close her eyes and sit up in bed. She sat surrounded by pillows as Petra, Sissy, and Marek marched into her room with her favorite breakfast. Laddy trailed behind and peeked over the bed.

"Happy Mother's Day, Mom!" the children said happily. Their mother was pleasantly surprised when she saw what her children had brought her. Later, she had a different kind of surprise when she saw the kitchen!

A gift for Franklin's father

Franklin's father was a business man. He wore a suit and worked in a tall office tower. He made big decisions and worked with important people. Franklin's father drove an expensive car and only wore silk ties. He had everything he wanted — or so Franklin thought. What could there be that Franklin could buy for Father's Day that his father might really like?

Suddenly, Franklin had a wonderful idea! He locked himself in his bedroom and worked hard for several hours. He made a card and wrote a poem in it for his father. He illustrated the card, too! Franklin could hardly wait to see his father's face when he gave him this Father's Day gift. He knew his father would smile one of his big, happy grins!

Father's Day

Father's Day was first celebrated in 1910. It falls on the third Sunday of June. Many people give their fathers cards and gifts on this day. Some fathers have quite a collection of ties as a result of Father's Day!

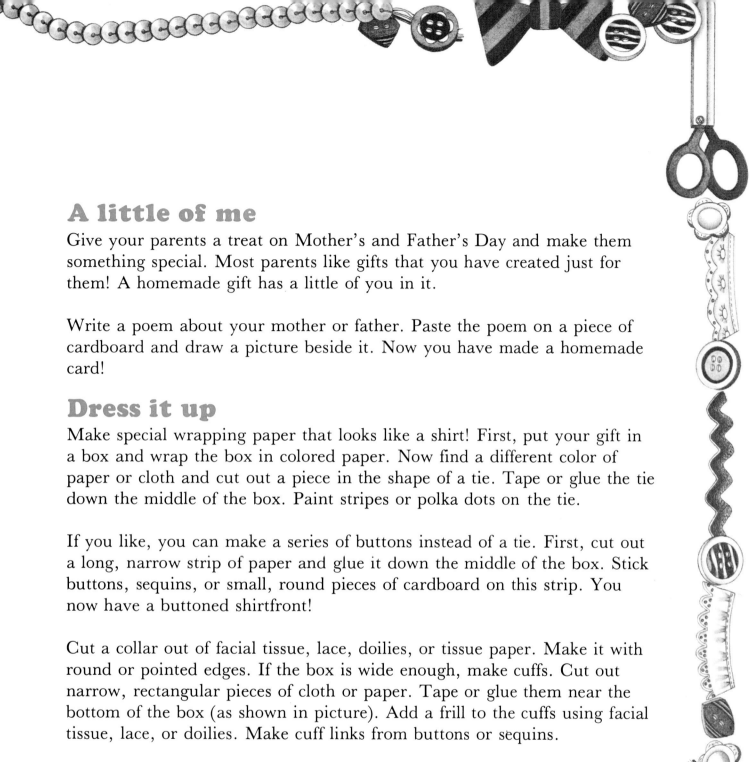

A little of me

Give your parents a treat on Mother's and Father's Day and make them something special. Most parents like gifts that you have created just for them! A homemade gift has a little of you in it.

Write a poem about your mother or father. Paste the poem on a piece of cardboard and draw a picture beside it. Now you have made a homemade card!

Dress it up

Make special wrapping paper that looks like a shirt! First, put your gift in a box and wrap the box in colored paper. Now find a different color of paper or cloth and cut out a piece in the shape of a tie. Tape or glue the tie down the middle of the box. Paint stripes or polka dots on the tie.

If you like, you can make a series of buttons instead of a tie. First, cut out a long, narrow strip of paper and glue it down the middle of the box. Stick buttons, sequins, or small, round pieces of cardboard on this strip. You now have a buttoned shirtfront!

Cut a collar out of facial tissue, lace, doilies, or tissue paper. Make it with round or pointed edges. If the box is wide enough, make cuffs. Cut out narrow, rectangular pieces of cloth or paper. Tape or glue them near the bottom of the box (as shown in picture). Add a frill to the cuffs using facial tissue, lace, or doilies. Make cuff links from buttons or sequins.

Your parents will be surprised by this beautiful wrapping. They may not want to ruin it by opening the boxes to find their gifts!

Girls' Day

In Japan, there are several family days which are special for children. Two of these days are Girls' Day and Boys' Day. Girls' Day is on March 3, the third day of the third month. Young girls dress in their best kimonos. Kimonos are loose robes tied with wide sashes. The girls take out their special Girls' Day dolls. They do not play with these dolls because the dolls are very old and fragile. They have been handed down from family member to family member for hundreds of years. There is an emperor and empress doll and other dolls that look like noble ladies. On Girls' Day, each home displays fifteen of these very old dolls in a special place.

The girls visit one another's homes to admire the doll collections. Rice cakes and tea are offered to the guests. Even the dolls get tiny cakes on tiny dishes!

My doll

See my doll,
See her smile,
She will sit and watch awhile.
While we eat cakes and sip tea,
She sits and watches and smiles at me!

Peach Blossom Festival

Another name for Girls' Day is the Peach Blossom Festival. Beside each display of dolls, there is a peach-blossom branch which reminds the girls to be thankful for the beauty in the world.

Sisterly love

Do you have a sister? Treat her in a special way on Girls' Day. Clean her room or leave a handmade bookmark by her breakfast plate. Go to the library, find a book that she wants to read, and leave it under her pillow. Make her a surprise snack when she gets home from school. If you do not have a sister, choose a female cousin or classmate for special treatment on this day.

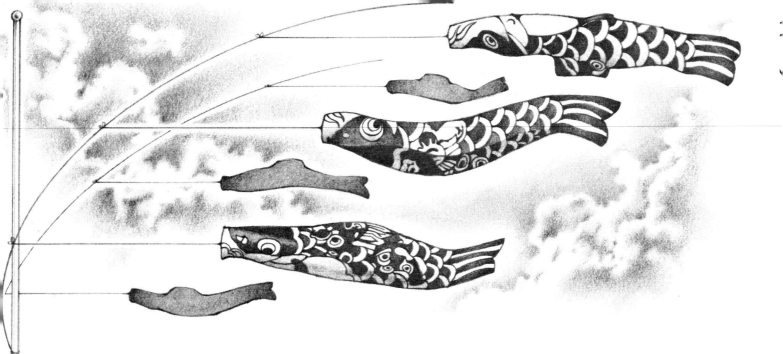

Boys' Day

There is a special day of celebration for Japanese boys, too. In Japan, Boys' Day is on May 5, the fifth day of the fifth month. The sky is filled with kites. The paper or cloth kites are in the shape of fish called carp. The carp is a strong fish. It swims up rivers against the current in order to lay its eggs. The carp kites remind the boys to be strong and determined when facing challenges in life. They are tied to bamboo poles outside each home. The number of kites which fly outside a home show people how many boys live in that home.

Ancient customs

Japanese boys have very old dolls that are dressed as samurai or special warriors. The boys display their dolls on Boys' Day, just as the girls display theirs on Girls' Day!

Iris leaves are part of the Boys' Day celebrations. Have you ever seen iris leaves? They are pointed and look like swords. Iris leaves are believed to drive away sickness. On the evening of Boys' Day, boys take hot baths with iris leaves in the water. The boys also eat rice balls wrapped in iris leaves.

14

A day for brothers and sisters

In India, Hindus celebrate a five-day festival called Diwali. The third day of Diwali is a special day for brothers and sisters. In the morning, the sister lights two lamps. Using red powder, she puts a *tika* or mark on her brother's forehead. This is to wish her brother a long and happy life.

Raksha Bandhan

Raksha Bandhan is another special celebration for Hindu brothers and sisters. It is held in August. The sister buys or makes a bracelet with colored threads, ribbons, or glittering paper. The bracelet is called a *rakhi.*

In the morning, the sister brings her brother a tray of fruit and sweets. She ties the rakhi around her brother's wrist. The bracelet confirms that the brother will protect and defend his sister. The sister puts a tika of red or yellow powder on her brother's forehead to bless him. The brother gives his sister gifts or money. The gifts and the bracelet remind the sister and brother of the love they have for each other.

Do you have a brother or sister? If a boy or girl in India has no brother or sister, he or she may choose a friend with whom to celebrate these holidays. This chosen friend becomes an honorary member of the family.

Grandparents' Days

In the United States, a special day has been set aside to celebrate grandparents. It is the first Sunday after Labor Day in September. Children give cards to their grandparents. They take their grandparents out for a special meal. Do you celebrate Grandparents' Day? Choose one day each month to visit, phone, or write to your grandparents and get to know them better!

Thoughts about grandparents

When you think of your grandparents, what pops into your mind? Read these thoughts about grandparents and then write your own!

My grandmother loves to jog. She gets up every morning at six and runs for half an hour. Then she fixes me breakfast and gives me a hug before I go to school.

When I visit my grandfather, we really have fun. We sometimes go shopping or feed the pigeons in the park. Sometimes we imagine we are on the moon. We talk moon talk. My mother thinks we are both a little strange.

My mom works. I like to go to my grandmother's apartment after school because I don't like being alone at home. My grandmother always has a snack ready. We sit down together, and I tell her all about school. She listens to every detail.

My grandmother taught me how to enjoy quiet. Sometimes we sit together for hours and never talk. She knits and I read. She is the most peaceful person I know.

My grandparents travel a lot. They bring me things from the places they visit. Sometimes they bring me T-shirts that I can't wear. They always forget my size!

My grandfather likes to sing. He has a terrible voice. I don't mind. I have a terrible voice, too. I sing with him. The dog barks. The cat yowls. My father thinks we should make a record.

My grandmother grows things. She has at least fifty plants. But that's not all she grows. She grows bean sprouts and sneaks them into my sandwiches.

Stages of life

You grow and change, and so does your family! Your mother may get a new job. Your grandfather may die. You may adopt a new baby sister. Your cousin may graduate from college. Your brother may get married. Your father may have a birthday.

Everyone is different and leads a special life, but most people pass through similar periods in life as they grow and change. Everyone begins life as a baby. When a new baby becomes part of a family, family members celebrate this happy event. The first day of school is an important day, too. On this day, it is time to enter a world full of new things to learn and experience. It is the beginning of a new stage in life and a time for a family to celebrate! A birthday, a graduation, a new job, and a marriage are also times to celebrate. A death is a time when a family wants to be together to remember the life of the family member who has just died.

Around the world

In every country of the world, people celebrate the different times of life. People around the world celebrate birth, the naming of babies, birthdays, reaching adulthood, marriage, and death. The ways of celebration may be different from country to country, but family feelings are the same.

Your important stages

What important stages have you had in your life?
— When were you born?
— When did you get your first tooth?
— At what age did you take your first steps?

— How old were you when you began to talk?

— Do you remember your first birthday? Your second? Your third?

— When did you begin school?

— When did you first learn to ride a tricycle or a bicycle?

Looking into the future

Can you think of other important times or stages in your life? Make a list and compare it with the lists of your friends. Can you think of future times that will be important in your life? Perhaps they will include the first day of high school, your graduation, the first time you vote in an election, the day you move away from your parents' home, or the day you get your first job.

The start of something new

A new baby is the start of a new life. Babies come in all shapes and sizes. Some have big ears and some have small ears. Some have hair and some are bald. It's exciting to see how quickly babies change as the days go by. Not one of these tiny human beings will be quite like any other human being in the world. No wonder babies are special.

Who needs a baby? Not me!

Sometimes it takes time to get used to the idea of having a new member of the family. John enjoyed being the only child in his family. Have you ever felt the way John did?

Father:

Wake up John, it's time to go,
Today's the happy day, you know.
Your mother just called on the phone to say
We will bring your baby sister home today.

John:

I don't want to go, I've made up my mind,
I don't want a baby of any kind!
Especially a sister, who needs that?
I would much prefer a hamster or a cat.

Father:

Don't be silly, you'll love her a lot,
There is nothing more fun than a little tot.
She'll squirm and fidget and roll and wiggle,
She'll smile and coo and make you giggle.

John:

But you and Mom will spend all your time
Watching her crawl, and walk, and climb.
We won't play ball, we won't go skating,
You'll play with her, while I sit here waiting.

Mom will cancel all the plans we had,
And so will you. Just think of it, Dad.
Because of the baby, I'll be forgotten,
I'll sit all alone and feel just rotten.

22

Father:

We'll have good times, just as before,
We'll do those things and even more.
We'll play ball and go camping, too,
We'll ride our bikes and go to the zoo!

Your sister is now part of our family, son,
Together you'll have hours and hours of fun.
She'll trust you, she'll need you, she'll love you so,
She'll follow behind you wherever you go.

John:

Let's leave now, Dad, don't make me wait.
I have a new sister, we can't be late.
To be a big brother is an important task!
What my sister's name? I forgot to ask.

Welcome to the world!

There are many ways to welcome a baby to the world. In Thailand, a new baby's foot is touched to the ground three times. People believe that this will help the baby to grow up healthy and strong. When a baby is put into the cradle for the first time, special objects are also placed in the cradle. It is believed that little bags of rice will help the baby to grow up wealthy. A pencil and notebook may be put in the cradle to help the baby do well at school.

Who are you?

One important way to welcome a baby to the world is to present him or her with a name. Have you ever noticed how important your name is? When you meet people you do not know, they want to know your name and you want to know their names. It is rare to meet someone with exactly the same first and last name as yours.

Quite a name!

Horatio Heffalump Hectabus Hoo
Was given his name before he turned two.
For such a small boy, that's quite a long name.
I think that his parents were largely to blame!

Baby's Day

In many countries, the naming of a baby is an important occasion. It is a time for the family to celebrate! In Japan, babies are named on Baby's Day. This day is celebrated about a month after the baby is born. The grandmother takes the baby to the temple. There, the baby is given a name. Later, everyone is invited to a feast. Gifts are presented to the baby. Toy dogs are a popular gift because everyone hopes that the baby will grow as fast as a puppy does!

Which one?

In parts of Egypt, four candles are lit during the naming ceremony. Each candle is given a name. Everyone waits until all but one candle burns out. The name of the candle that burns the longest is given to the baby!

Christening

Many Christian families baptize or christen their children. At the christening, water is sprinkled on the baby's head, or the baby is dipped in water three times. The child is now a member of the church and is given a name.

Often, the parents have chosen two friends to be the godparents of their baby. The godparents promise that they will help the child to become a good Christian. The godparents become a part of the family!

What's in a name?

How did you get your name? Most people have at least two names. Some people have as many as five or six. Your first name is your given name. Family names or last names are called surnames. A second or middle name comes between the first and last name.

Given names

Parents often name their babies after themselves or other family members. If the father's name is Wally, the baby might be named Wally Junior. A baby girl might be named after her mother, aunt, grandmother, or even her grandfather! If her grandfather's name is Don, the girl might be called "Dawn." People also name their children after saints, friends, important people in government, or movie stars. Some parents invent new names for their children.

Discovering surnames

Where did surnames come from? A long time ago, not many people lived together in one area or village, and most people had only one name. As the number of people living in one place grew, many children ended up having the same names. So, if there were two boys named Ron, people would distinguish them by saying whose son they were. One boy would be called, "Ron, John's son" and the other boy, "Ron, Peter's son." "John's son" became the surname Johnson. "Peter's son" became the surname Peterson. In this way, the father's given name (John or Peter) became part of his son's surname! Guess which given names these surnames came from: Davidson, Dickson, Williamson, and Fredrickson.

Sometimes only an "s" was added to the father's name to form a surname. Adam's son or daughter received the surname Adams. In the Spanish language, "ez" was added to a given name. Martinez means "Martin's child." In Italian, "de" was put in front of some names. "De" means "of." De Stefano means "of Stephen" or "Stephen's child."

Names that tell a story

Surnames also came from types of work. People might refer to Carl as "the baker." Soon Baker would be Carl's surname. Other surnames that came from types of work are Singer, Taylor (from tailor), Smith (from blacksmith), and Merchant.

Surnames sometimes described people. Mrs. Small might have been a tiny woman. Mr. Long was probably tall. What might Mr. Beard have looked like? Surnames also described where people lived. Some people lived near a hill, a wall, water, a field, or in an orchard. Their surnames might be Hill, Wall, Atwater, Field, or Crabtree.

What do they mean?

Some non-English surnames can be translated into English. Boulanger is the French word for baker. Grossman is the German word for tall man. Is your surname non-English? Can you translate it into English?

Spanish naming customs

In countries where people speak Spanish, a person's middle name is the same as his or her father's middle name. A person's last name is the same as his or her mother's middle name. Here is an example: Enrique Martinez Mompel and Mercedes Lopez Corres have a child, Raul. Raul's full name will be Raul Martinez (father's middle name) Lopez (mother's middle name). If you were to follow this naming custom, what would your full name be? To answer this question, you must know your parents' middle names.

Do you have a middle name? Find out if your middle name has a special meaning. It may not! Perhaps your parents chose the name because it sounded pleasant between your other names!

Names all around

Look at the border on this page. Do you see your name here? Do you see the names of any of your friends?

Name Days

In some countries, Christian parents sometimes name their children after saints. Saints are people who are honored by the Christian church because they devoted their lives to doing good deeds. Each saint in the church has a special day on which he or she is remembered and honored.

Agnes is my name

I was born on Saint Agnes' Day. That is why my parents called me Agnes. Saint Agnes' Day is my birthday and my Name Day. We celebrate on this day! Sometimes, though, I wish I was born on Saint Catherine's Day. I like the name Catherine better than the name Agnes!

Two celebrations!

My name is John. I was named after Saint John because he is my parents' favorite saint. This means that my Name Day is the day of Saint John. I was not born on Saint John's Day, though. I celebrate my birthday on the day that I was born. I have two celebrations every year, just for me!

Happy Name Day!

In Greece, children go to church on their Name Day. They honor the saint after whom they have been named. All day long, friends and neighbors bring gifts to the child. The child is treated to his or her favorite desserts. Later in the day, there is a special dinner for the Name Day child.

Who am I?

This is a perfect game for a Name Day party. Every player has a paper pinned on his or her back with the name of a famous person or character written on it. The players do not know their own new names, but they can read everyone else's name. The players move about and talk to one another as if they are talking to the famous characters or people. Each player tries to discover his or her new name by picking up clues from what the other players say to them!

Happy birthday

Happy birthday to you,
Happy birthday to you,
Happy birthday, dear Angela,
Happy birthday to you!

Have you heard this Happy Birthday song before? It was written by two American women more than sixty years ago. Now it is sung in many countries around the world.

Come to a party

People celebrate birthdays all over the world. In North America and Europe, there are birthday parties. Let's watch people as they celebrate. Here come the guests, dressed in their best clothes. They are bringing gifts to the birthday person. Can you see the flicker of tiny candle flames? Everyone sings Happy Birthday. With a big puff, the birthday person tries to blow out all the candles on the cake!

Candles, wishes, and prayers

Thousands of years ago, the Romans and Greeks believed that their gods liked to see candle flames, so they lit candles to please them. Candles have been special ever since. The Germans were the first people to put candles on birthday cakes. Do you believe that if you make a wish and blow out all the candles, your birthday wish will come true?

What will the future hold?

In China, a baby has a birthday celebration when he or she is thirty days old. The baby has another birthday at the end of his or her first year. This is called the One Year Celebration. The baby is set on a table and different objects are placed in front of him or her. The family and guests watch to see which object the baby will touch first. They believe that the choice of the object will tell them about the baby's future. If a baby touches a book, he or she will be a scholar. If the baby touches a compass, he or she will love traveling.

Other important ages

In the countries of the East, elderly people have a place of honor in the family. They are respected for their experience and wisdom. That is why the sixtieth and seventieth birthday celebrations are important ones for the Chinese. The whole family gathers to honor the birthday person. The grandchildren can't wait to give their grandparent gifts, hugs, and kisses.

A happy birthday?

As soon as Jennifer woke up, she had a smile on her face and butterflies in her stomach. She knew this day was a special one, but she could not remember why. She tried to roll over and go back to sleep. It was impossible! "Oh yes!" she remembered suddenly. "It is my birthday today, and I nearly forgot!"

In a flash, Jennifer jumped out of bed and into her clothes. She rushed downstairs. Her parents and her two brothers were just beginning to eat breakfast. When she sat down at the table, everyone looked up at her and said, "Good morning, Jennifer." Then they went back to eating, talking, and reading the newspaper. Jennifer almost blurted out, "Hey, it's my birthday!" but she stopped herself. Surely they would soon remember.

She played alone in her room all morning. She knew that by lunchtime her parents and brothers would remember that today was her birthday. But when lunch was over, they got up from the table and moved away in different directions.

Jennifer was starting to get worried now. "Can I go with you, Pat and Rick?" she asked her brothers.

"Sorry," they said quickly. "We're going to see our friend, Ralph, and you can't come." They ran off.

"What are you doing today, Dad? Can I do it with you?" asked Jennifer.

"I have to work at the store today. No time to play." He hurried out the door.

"How about you, Mom?" asked Jennifer. "Can we do something together?"

"I must finish some work at the office. Sorry, but I have to do it today." She rushed off.

Jennifer felt unhappy and disappointed. What an awful birthday she was having. No one was paying any attention to her. No one remembered it was her special day. She tried to force back her tears.

Suddenly, she had an idea. She knew that she could always count on her grandmother when she had a problem. Her grandmother made her feel like the most special person in the whole world. She never forgot anything. Surely she would remember that it was Jennifer's birthday!

Jennifer ran out of the house, but soon she slowed down to a walk. What if her grandmother had also forgotten that today was her special day? Her grandmother lived only two blocks away, but it took Jennifer a long time to get to her house. She stood in front of her door for a few minutes. What if Granny had forgotten her birthday, too? She knocked on the door. No one answered. She knocked again. Still no answer. Maybe her grandmother was not even home! Jennifer knocked one last time. This time, Granny opened the door.

She looked surprised to see Jennifer. She did not even say ''Happy birthday.'' She invited Jennifer in and told her to go and wait in the living room. Jennifer was so unhappy that she could hardly move. Even Granny had forgotten her birthday! She walked slowly down the hallway to the dark living room. She reached up and flicked on the light switch.

Surprise!

Suddenly, the room was filled with colors, whistles, and shouts. Jennifer saw balloons and streamers. "Surprise! Happy birthday, Jennifer!" Her whole family and many of her friends crowded around her. Jennifer's mouth fell open. "I thought you had all forgotten my birthday," she finally managed to say.

"What? Forget your birthday? Never!" her father cried. "We only pretended to because we wanted to surprise you, and it sure looks like we did."

Games, food, and gifts

Jennifer's party was a real surprise! Have you ever had a surprise birthday party? It's hard to keep a party secret because everyone wants to burst out with the exciting news.

There are lots of ways to have fun at birthday parties! In Hawaii, there is a special birthday meal of roast beef, fish, bananas, and papaya. In Russia, a birthday pie has the name of the birthday child cut into the crust before it is baked. At birthday celebrations in Iran, the children hide the gifts they bring. The birthday child must go on a treasure hunt. What a fun way to receive birthday presents! In Germany, the birthday child comes to the breakfast table in the morning and finds his or her chair piled high with gifts.

Your own birthday traditions

How do you celebrate your birthday? Do you have special foods that you like to eat? Do you have a party? Compare your birthday traditions with those of your friends.

First days

The first day of anything is always exciting because it offers a lot of new experiences. This makes first days a little scary, but also a lot of fun. You will have many first days in your life. Your first day of school is just one of them!

Your first day of school

Let's talk about that special day — your first day of school! People in your family share your excitement. They wish they could be in the classroom with you, but this is something you must do alone. This is your day.

Do you remember?

Did you feel happy or frightened on your first day of school? Perhaps you felt a little of both. What did you wear? How did you get to school? Were you driven to school in a car or a bus? Did you walk? Who walked with you to show you the way?

Do you remember the name of your first teacher? Was it exciting to meet him or her? Was your teacher excited about meeting all the new students?

Tell us more

Another important part of the first day of school was meeting all your classmates. Did you already know some of the children in your class, or were they all new to you? Are some of the children you met that day still your friends?

Can you remember what you did on your first day of school? Did you learn everyone's name? Did you play outside at recess? Did you begin learning new things? What did you learn? Were you glad or sorry when your first day of school was over?

German first-day cones

In Germany, the child who is going to school for the first time is given a large paper cone. The child's parents fill it with candies and cookies.

Make a first-day cone for a younger brother, sister, or friend who is beginning school. Cut a large piece of stiff paper or cardboard into a square. Draw a line that curves from one corner to the opposite corner. Cut along the line. Roll the straight edges of the paper or cardboard together, so that the edges overlap.

Line the inside of the cone with crepe paper. Let the crepe paper frill out over the top of the cone. Decorate the cone with pieces of colored paper, or make a design on it with crayons or markers. Fill the cone with candies and little gifts. Carefully tie the crepe paper shut with a ribbon. The ribbon will hold the treats inside until the first-day child wants to enjoy them.

Hurray for kids!

Leap up high,
Touch the sky,
Clap your hands,
Do headstands.

Ride a cloud,
Sing out loud,
Kids are great
So celebrate!

I'm glad to be a child!

What would it be like if all children celebrated their birthdays on the same day? It would be a day of fun and laughter. It might be like Children's Day!

The dragon game

In Indonesia, Children's Day is in June. Children sing and play a dragon game. They walk in a line, each holding the waist of the child in front. This line is the dragon. The children sing:

See the dragon long and fierce,
Terrible is he.
Here and there he twists and turns,
As you all can see.
Prey that's good to eat he seems to lack.
Here he's found it too, at the very back!

When the song is finished, the child at the beginning of the line (the dragon's head) tries to catch the child at the end of the line (the dragon's tail). The twisting dragon spins and dances. Everyone hangs on tightly! If the tail is caught or lets go of the line, this end player must leave the game. The game begins again with a shorter dragon and continues until there are only two children left!

Reward yourself

Do you celebrate Children's Day? Do you think that children deserve a special day? Think of some reasons why children are great. Celebrate your own Children's Day with your friends. What activities will you have? What games will you play? How will you reward yourself for being a great kid?

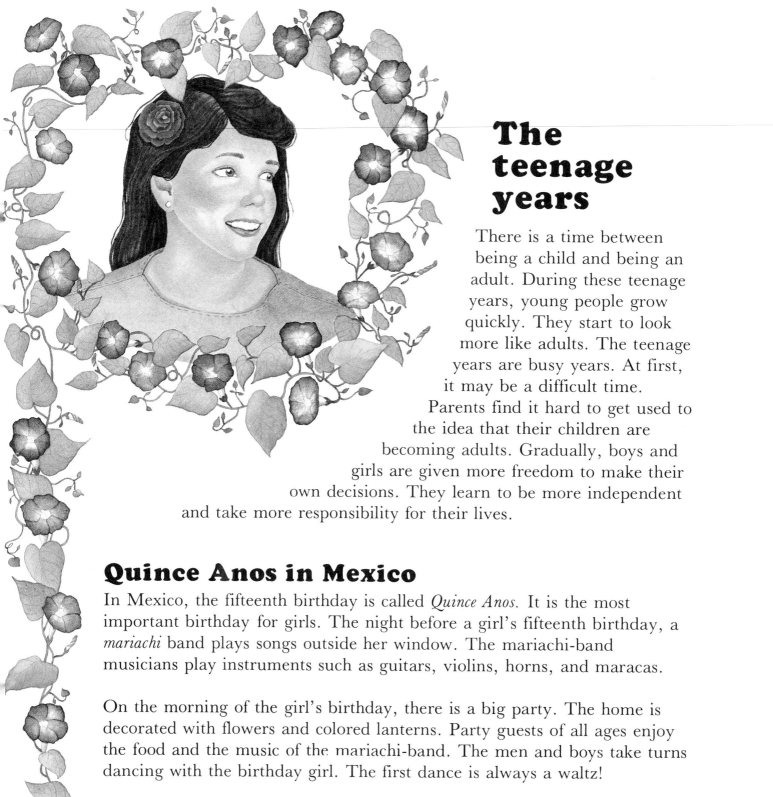

The teenage years

There is a time between being a child and being an adult. During these teenage years, young people grow quickly. They start to look more like adults. The teenage years are busy years. At first, it may be a difficult time. Parents find it hard to get used to the idea that their children are becoming adults. Gradually, boys and girls are given more freedom to make their own decisions. They learn to be more independent and take more responsibility for their lives.

Quince Anos in Mexico

In Mexico, the fifteenth birthday is called *Quince Anos*. It is the most important birthday for girls. The night before a girl's fifteenth birthday, a *mariachi* band plays songs outside her window. The mariachi-band musicians play instruments such as guitars, violins, horns, and maracas.

On the morning of the girl's birthday, there is a big party. The home is decorated with flowers and colored lanterns. Party guests of all ages enjoy the food and the music of the mariachi-band. The men and boys take turns dancing with the birthday girl. The first dance is always a waltz!

The passing of knowledge

Some Africans and North American Indians have special growing-up ceremonies for boys and girls. Before these ceremonies, the boys or girls usually live away from their tribes for several days. They are taught the secrets of the tribe and the ways of the adults. After they are brought back into the tribe, they are treated as adults.

Confirmation

Many Christian boys and girls go to special classes to learn more about the Bible and the rules of their churches. Then they take part in a special ceremony called confirmation. The bishop or minister puts holy oil on their foreheads. This is believed to ''confirm'' or strengthen the young people's ties with God.

Bat and bar mitzvahs

Jewish girls at the age of twelve have a celebration called *bat mitzvah*. Boys have a similar celebration soon after their thirteenth birthday. It is called a *bar mitzvah*. Both boys and girls must learn a great deal about their religion at this stage of their lives. Read about David's bar mitzah.

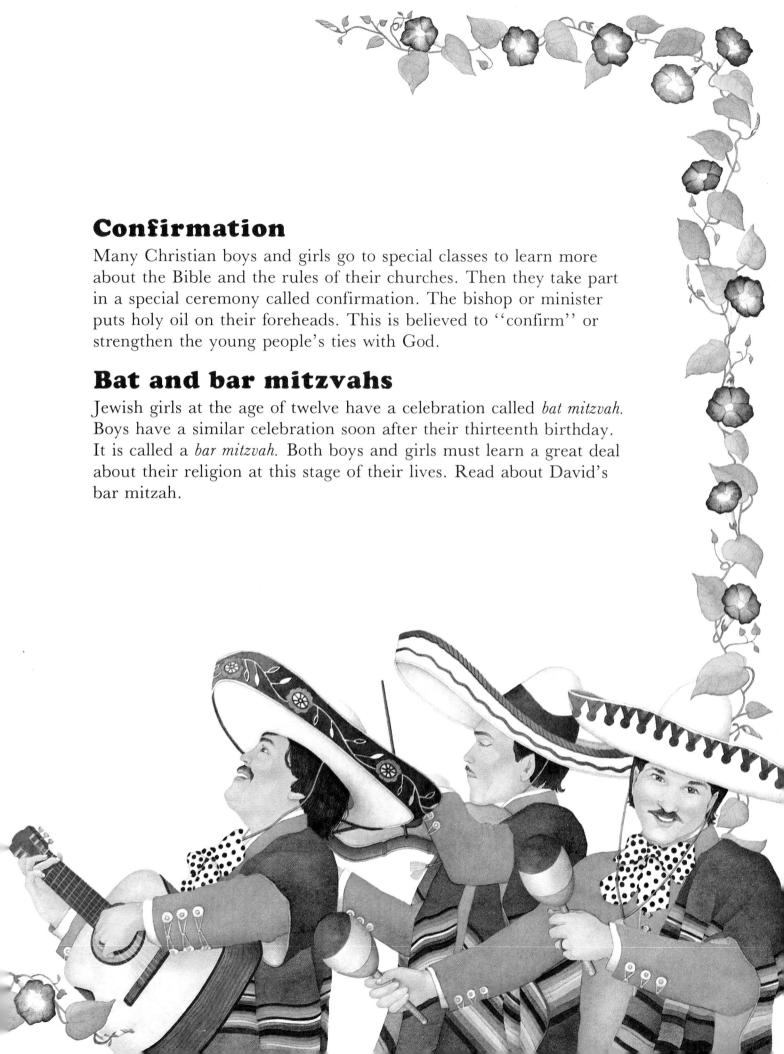

David's Bar Mitzvah

David was very nervous as he put on his new suit. His hands shook so much that he could hardly tie the laces on his shiny, polished shoes. Today was one of the most important days in David's life. David was thirteen, and today was his bar-mitzvah ceremony. This ceremony would show that he was an adult in the Jewish community. He would have greater responsibilities at the synagogue, the Jewish house of worship.

David's sister, Deborah, came into his room. "You'd better hurry," she told him. "We don't want to be late for your bar mitzvah."

This made David more nervous. He tried to hurry, but his hands shook even more.

Deborah smiled at her brother. "Don't worry, David," she said. "You've been preparing for a whole year. You've learned the Hebrew language and your teacher has spent many hours teaching you about our holy book, the Torah. You've practiced your reading and memorized your speech. You'll do fine, David."

"Were you this nervous at your bat mitzvah?" David asked his sister.

"Of course I was nervous," said Deborah. "But even so, I only made one small mistake." She hugged her brother. "Don't worry so much!"

David and his family arrived at the synagogue. David's father placed a prayer shawl or *tallis* around David's shoulders. As he walked up the center aisle, David saw many of his friends and relatives crowding the benches. "So many people! What if I make a mistake?" David thought. He tried to concentrate on the ceremony that was just beginning.

The cantor or chief singer of the synagogue began to sing. The Torah scrolls were placed on the reading table. Now David had to show how hard he had been working for the last several months. His stomach was fluttering and his knees felt weak when he stood up. His hands were shaking. He could see that everyone was looking at him and waiting.

Then David began to read. Suddenly, he realized that his voice was steady and loud. His hands stopped shaking. His legs were strong. He read the Hebrew verses and then spoke to the members of the synagogue. He told them how much his bar mitzvah meant to him. He thanked his family and relatives, his teacher, and the rabbi for all their help. He had not forgotten one word of the speech that he had memorized.

Before he knew it, the ceremony was over and he was home again. People gave him gifts and wished him luck. They praised him for the fine job he had done.

David found himself in front of a huge bar-mitzvah cake. There were many candles on it. His mother, father, sister, grandparents, aunts, uncles, and cousins each lit one candle. Then a knife was placed in David's hand and he was asked to cut the cake.

"This is the easiest part of the ceremony," David thought happily as he held the knife. Suddenly, his hand began to shake. His stomach had butterflies in it. His knees felt weak. The pieces of cake that David cut were jagged and messy! David laughed, and everybody else laughed along with him.

Weddings help families grow!

Everyone looks forward to weddings. Weddings are the start of new families. Weddings also join two families into one big family. This is why they are such important family celebrations! There are many different wedding customs around the world. Let's look at a wedding in India.

Sarita and Shiv, the bride and groom

Sarita and Shiv are getting married. The festivities begin the night before the wedding at Sarita's home. Sarita's sisters and brothers present Shiv's mother with colorful saris. A *sari* is an Indian dress. It is a long piece of silk or other colorful material that is wrapped around the waist and pulled over the shoulder. Shiv's family gives Sarita necklaces, earrings, and nose-rings for her to wear at the wedding. Shiv presents Sarita with wedding rings.

More gift-giving!

The gift-giving continues on the morning of the wedding. Sarita's eldest brother takes gifts to Shiv. While Shiv receives his gifts, Sarita's sisters and female guests visit the bride-to-be for the *mehndi* ritual. Delicate designs are painted on their palms and feet with a reddish dye. Many Hindus believe that the color red brings good luck and happiness. The designs show that the event is an important one.

44

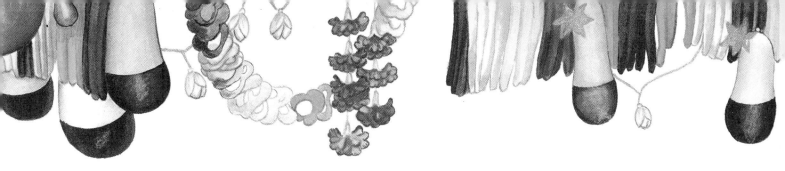

Preparing for the wedding

The women help Sarita prepare for her wedding. They dress her in a red sari embroidered in gold. They help her decorate her home with lights, flowers, streamers, and balloons. Everything is now ready for the wedding celebration.

Shiv arrives

In the evening, Shiv travels to Sarita's home on a white horse decorated with a brightly-colored cloth, headdress, feathers, jewels, and flowers. Shiv is wearing a colorful turban on his head and his dark suit is brightened with jewelry. Sarita welcomes him with a garland of flowers. The guests throw flower petals at the happy couple. Then everyone enjoys a meal of rich foods.

The seven promises

Shiv makes seven promises to Sarita. He says: ''I promise to keep you happy. I will share my feelings with you and share everything I own with you. I will be faithful to you and respect your family. I now make you part of my life.'' The seventh promise Shiv makes is a promise to keep all of these six promises!

Sarita accepts Shiv as her husband. She is happy because she is now part of a new family. Shiv is happy because he is part of Sarita's family. It is exciting to think that the young couple may also start a family of their own.

Traditional or not?

There are many kinds of wedding ceremonies. Some of them are religious and some of them are not. Sometimes a couple follows a particular ceremony which many other couples have followed. This is called a traditional wedding. Sometimes couples make up their own ceremonies.

Family words

teenager

bar mitzvah

candles

birthday cake

Torah

tallis

father/
stepfather

brother/stepbrother

grandfather

mother/stepmother/aunt

toddler

cousin

grandmother

uncle

cousin

baby

sister/stepsister

carp kite

sari

mehndi

grandchild

paper cone

groom

bride

wedding

47

Times of change

Families get together to say hello to a new member of the family. They also get together to say good-bye. Often these are sad times. A family member may become divorced or move to another country. A family member may die. Saying good-bye is difficult, but getting together to say good-bye helps people to accept changes in life. It is a good time to remember happy times in the past and to realize how important each member of the family is. It is a good time to say a special hello to all the members who are gathered together!

Once again!

An anniversary is an event that happened on the same date in an earlier year. There are many kinds of anniversaries. A wedding aniversary is a popular family celebration. It is celebrated every year on the same date that the wedding was celebrated. The married couple and their family remember the promises that the couple made to each other. The couple celebrates their marriage again!

A time for us

Some people work hard for many years and then retire or leave their jobs. Many people must retire from their jobs when they reach a certain age. Others retire when they feel they have earned a rest and enough money to afford a rest! Retiring from work is an important stage in a person's life. It can be a difficult time. It is hard to get used to the change of no longer working every day. What will the person choose to do with his or her time? Maybe he will spend more time with his family. Maybe she will relax or start another job!

A new beginning

Some families have parties to celebrate a family member's retirement. Many of the people who have worked with the family member come to the retirement party. They say, "Thank you for helping our days at work to be successful and fun. We will miss you." They may give gifts to show how they feel. They are sad that they will no longer see their friend every day, but everyone wants to celebrate the new life that the retired person is about to begin. Everyone says, "Good luck and much happiness!"

49

A family activity

Do you spend much time with your family? Do you talk together or play any favorite games? Why not start an exciting project the whole family can work on!

A family newspaper

Start your own family newspaper and send it to all your relatives. You can publish it once a year or several times a year, if you like! It is a fun way to keep in touch with family members that you do not see very often.

Have a family meeting and talk about new family events. Did your mother or father get a new job? Has your family been on vacation? Has someone moved to a new home? Write up any items of interest. Each person can contribute something. Don't forget photographs, pictures, poems, and stories!

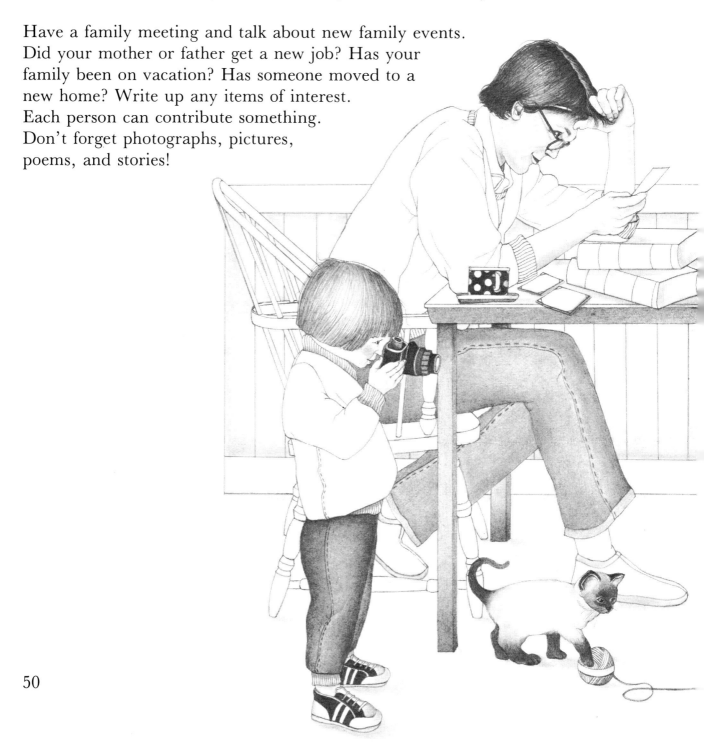

Divide your newspaper into sections, such as Business (work, school), Travel (vacations), Food (family recipes), and Entertainment (stories, movie reviews, family jokes). Ask relatives to send you any stories they wish to share. Your newspaper can grow and grow with the help of out-of-town correspondents!

When it is ready, photocopy the newspaper and send one copy to each of your relatives. Don't forget to save copies for your family scrapbook!

52

One big family

Hey, hey! You're okay!
Here is what I've got to say:
You've got a family. *Yes, I know.*
And you've got one more! *How's that so?*

You're a member of the world family:
Everyone here, as far as you can see.
What's that family? How can it be?
I've just got Grandma, Dad, Sis, and me!

Listen to me now and I'll tell you true.
Rattle your bones and shake your shoe.
The family of people is you and me
And everyone here and across the sea!

That's a lot of people. Yet you say
We're all related — in what way?
Biddle boddle bong. Open your eyes.
Ring rottle tot. It's no surprise!

We're all peoplc. That's all we need
To be one family. *Yes, indeed.*
We're all ages, all shapes, every size.
Touch your toes and tickle the skies.

I like my new family. Say hey, hey.
Splash in the stream and waddle my way.
Now come along and don't be late,
We're having a party to celebrate!

Sing laddi-la and sing lady-lay,
Stand up, sit down, March, April, May.
Whistle up a storm and float on a cloud,
We're one family — Shout it out loud!

53

great-grandfather

great-grandmother

great-grandfather

great-grandmother

grandmother

grandfather

aunts
uncles

father

cousins

me
brothers
sisters

A family tree

This family tree shows how you are related to the members of your family. Copy it or design your own, and put the names of your family members in the correct spaces.

great-grandfather

great-grandmother

great-grandfather

great-grandmother

grandfather

grandmother

mother

aunts
uncles

cousins

Your family tree belongs to the forest of family trees around the world. Make this forest a beautiful, peaceful place to be! Celebrate families everywhere!

55

Index

56

567890LB Printed in the USA 987654